Contents

Chapter 1
The Race

A cold, wet nose pressed against Zeb's cheek.

"Get off, Nukka!" Zeb said.

Nukka wagged her tail. She was happy.
She was Zeb's best husky dog and she knew
it. She could get away with a lot.

Zeb had got Nukka when she was a puppy.
Nukka means 'little sister'. She made Zeb
think of a cheeky little sister who chased
him around all day. She never got tired. She
liked to poke her nose into everything. She
liked to boss the other dogs about.

Zeb was 15. He lived in Anchorage, a
small town in Alaska. Alaska is part of the
USA. It is next to Canada and it's a very cold
place.

There are two main sports in Alaska – ice hockey and dog sledding. Zeb didn't like ice hockey, but he loved dog sledding. When the sky was blue and the air was cold, going sledding was the best thing in the world.

Zeb had 8 dogs to pull his sled. He stood on the sled and rode behind them. Nukka was the lead dog out in front.

Years ago, in the days before cars and snow-mobiles, dog sledding was not just a sport. It was the only way of getting about on snow and ice. In 1925, hundreds of people in the town of Nome fell ill. They needed medicine fast, but no car was able to drive over the snow and frozen ice, so they had to use sleds. Men and dogs used sleds to bring medicine the 674 miles back to Nome. They saved hundreds of lives.

Zeb had been told that story since he was a baby.

"We could sled that far too, Nukka," Zeb said. "Easy." Nukka wagged her tail. "We could do more than that," Zeb told her.

Zeb's dream was to race his dogs on the Iditarod trail, the hardest dog race in the world. The race was 1,149 miles across snow and ice. It was you and your dogs against the cold and ice. Alone.

The race was held to remember how the people of Nome were saved in 1925. The person who won was a hero.

"The prize money could buy Mum and Dad a nice house," Zeb said to Nukka.

Zeb was fed up with just dreaming of the Iditarod.

Chapter 2
Not for Kids

The Iditarod race took place every March. Four days before the start of the race, people and their dogs came from Alaska, Canada and from all over the world to Zeb's home town of Anchorage.

The men and women who drove the dog sleds were called 'mushers'. The name comes from the word 'mush' which means 'go' when you talk to huskies. 'Gee' means 'go right' and 'haw' means 'go left'. 'Whoa' means 'slow down'.

Zeb was good at mushing. He was proud to be such a young musher.

That March, Zeb and his dad watched all the mushers arrive.

"Look, Dad!" Zeb said. "There's Martin Buser. He's won four times! I thought he'd stopped racing now."

"I don't think old mushers ever stop racing," said Zeb's dad. "They just slide away."

"Ha, ha! That's funny, Dad. Don't you mean sled away?" Zeb joked.

Zeb waited a moment then he said, "Dad, can I ..."

"I know what you're going to say, Zeb," his dad said. "But my answer is still no. You're too young. You have to be 18 to race in the Iditarod. You're only 15 now. In three years' time we'll talk about it again."

"But, Dad ..."

"I said no." Zeb's dad walked away.

Zeb felt angry. The rules were unfair. He was just as good as these grown-up mushers – if not better.

"I could do the Iditarod now!" he yelled.

An old musher with a long, white beard shook his head. "Son, this race ain't for kids. It's hard. Real hard. You get it wrong and you die."

Another musher came over. "You listen to the old man, kid," he said. "This race isn't for babies. It's for adults. Stay home and do what your mum tells you."

Zeb's face was red as he walked away.

"I'll show them," he said to himself. "I'll show them all."

Chapter 3
Zeb's Secret Plan

That night Zeb made up his mind he would enter the Iditarod – no matter what anyone said.

"I'm not a kid. I'm as good as any of those mushers," he said to himself.

Zeb took his ID card and turned the '15' into an '18'. It was easy. "Now they'll have to let me race," he said to himself.

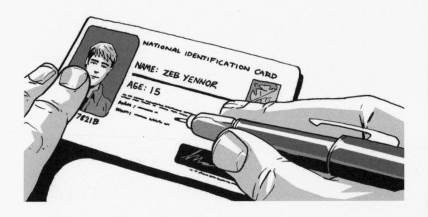

There was a lot to do before the race started. Zeb looked at the long list of things he needed.

Food for 3 weeks

Dog food for 8 dogs

Warm clothes

Sunglasses

Mini stove with fuel

Matches

Radio

Water

Sleeping bag

Tent

Gun and bullets

The list went on.

"And I mustn't forget I need 32 booties," Zeb said.

The booties weren't for Zeb. Each dog needed a set of 4 booties to cover its paws. Sharp ice could cut a dog's paws badly.

"I'll have to hide all this stuff or Mum and Dad will find it. No way would they let me race – or even leave the house – if they knew," Zeb told Nukka.

Zeb had only three days to make his plan work.

He hid his food and other things in a shed behind the house. No one went in there. It was full of old rubbish. His things would be safe.

The night before the race, Zeb was thinking about how his parents would feel when they found out that he'd gone.

"I'd better leave a note for Mum and Dad," he said to Nukka. "Once I'm on the trail they can't stop me, but I don't want them to worry."

Zeb wrote a note to his parents.

Dear Mum and Dad

You'll be shocked when you know where I've gone! I'm doing the Iditarod! Don't worry – Nukka will look after me. I promise I'll be safe and I'll be home soon.

Please don't be cross – I know I can do this.

Love
Zeb

Early the next morning, Zeb left the note on his bed.

"By the time Mum and Dad read this, I'll be gone," he said.

But when Zeb closed his bedroom door, the note blew off the bed. It landed under the bed, where there were lots of other bits of paper. Zeb's parents would never find the note now.

Chapter 4
Danger!

The man from the race looked at Zeb's ID.

"Are you sure you're 18, son?" he asked.

"Yes!" said Zeb. "Ten weeks ago."

"And you've got all the kit on the list? Your sled looks a bit light."

"I've got everything I need," Zeb said.

The man shook his head. "I can't stop you, son. If you have any problems, use your radio. OK?"

Zeb grinned. "I won't have any problems."

The man shook his head again and told Zeb to go to the start line.

More than 70 mushers and their dogs waited side by side at the start line.

"If Mum and Dad are here, they'll never spot me in this crowd," said Zeb. He felt a bit bad about his mum and dad, but he'd see them again soon.

The race began and the mushers set off. They took it slow at the start. But then they left the town behind. There was nothing before them but a world of white. Zeb's dogs picked up speed and ran over the snow. They loved this as much as he did.

Zeb's fast team of dogs and his light sled flew over the snow. All of a sudden he was in the lead!

The trail took Zeb into the silent forest. Nukka turned her head left and right. It was hard for her to see in the dim light.

"What's the matter, Nukka?" Zeb said.

Nukka gave a bark to warn him.

From out of the trees came a moose. It was a male with big, sharp antlers.

Zeb knew that a male moose was very heavy. One could weigh over half a ton. That's about the same as 10 men. And an angry moose could run up to 35 miles an hour. If its antlers didn't get you, a kick from one of its hooves could kill.

This moose wasn't happy to see them. It was hungry after a long winter, and it was in a bad temper. The moose hated people and it hated wolves. And Zeb's dogs looked like wolves.

The angry moose charged at Zeb.

"Mush! Mush!" Zeb yelled.

Nukka knew what to do. She turned away from the moose, and ran at top speed. The other dogs ran too. Fear made them very fast!

Zeb could hear the moose's angry bellow behind them.

The dogs ran and ran until they couldn't see or hear the moose any more.

"That was a bit too close," said Zeb. His voice was shaky. "Thanks, Nukka."

Chapter 5
Snow and Ice

Two weeks later, Zeb and his dogs had covered over 1,000 miles of snow and ice. The race was going well. The days were happy and full of joy. There were cosy cabins along the way where they spent the nights.

On Day 15, Zeb woke up and stretched. He could see his breath in the cold morning air.

Nukka stuck her nose into his pocket to look for a treat. He stroked her thick fur.

"Sorry, Nukka," he said. "I haven't got any treats. We're getting a bit low on food."

Nukka looked sad.

They set off in the sharp, clear light. The dogs were running well and the sled ride was smooth and fast.

'This is what dog sledding is all about,'
Zeb thought. 'A good team, a blue sky and
the end of the race just a few days away.'
Zeb knew that no one as young as him had
ever finished the Iditarod before.

But Zeb should have looked behind him.

A storm was coming. A smart musher
would make camp now, put up a tent and
shelter from the storm. Zeb had forgotten
the first rule of sledding – be ready for
anything.

All of a sudden, the wind was icy. Snow
was settling on the dogs' backs.

"I can't see the trail," said Zeb. He felt very nervous.

The storm raged around the sled. Snow like steel cut into Zeb's face. Zeb's dogs were running blind now. They were scared by the wild storm. Mushers called it a 'white out'. It was all Zeb could do to hold on to the sled. He could not feel his hands – his fingers were numb with cold.

"If I fall off the sled," he said to himself, "I'll be dead." In this weather, a person could freeze to death fast.

"I must stop the sled," said Zeb. "We could drive into a crevasse."

A crevasse is like a big crack in the thick ice – some are hundreds of feet deep. All mushers feared them. If you fell in, no one would ever find your body.

On most days, Zeb could shout "Whoa" and press the foot brake to slow the sled. Not today. The dogs were in a panic. Zeb would have to use the ice-hook. The ice-hook was a way of getting the dogs to turn or suddenly stop. "A bit like a hand-brake in a car," Zeb's dad had told him.

Zeb used all his strength to slam the iron ice-hook into the icy ground with his left hand. The sled started to tip over and Zeb cried out. He threw himself to the right. "I must keep the sled up!" he shouted.

Too late.

The heavy sled crashed down on its side.

Zeb was thrown clear.

He lay in the snow and didn't move.

Water freezes at 0°C. At minus 44°C, skin freezes in less than a minute. Warm clothes keep you safe for up to half an hour. But no one was coming to help Zeb. He was on his own. Apart from Nukka. She ran to him and licked his face.

Chapter 6
All Alone ...

The storm raged all day and all night. Zeb's
8 dogs huddled around him. Without the
heat of their bodies, he would have frozen to
death.

In the pale morning light, Zeb woke up.
He groaned in pain and Nukka licked his face.
Zeb tried to sit up, but pain stabbed through

him. It hurt to breathe. Perhaps he had broken a rib, or even two or three?

"We can't go on, Nukka," Zeb said. "I must radio for help. My parents are going to kill me."

Zeb stood up slowly. He was in great pain. He swore and held his ribs. Very slowly, he pulled the sled the right way up. He got the radio out of his pack. Then his mouth went dry. The radio was broken. Useless.

"This is really bad news," Zeb said.

Nukka licked his hand.

Zeb had no choice. He had to go on by himself.

He fed the dogs what little food was left. He opened a tin of beans for himself. It was frozen solid and Zeb's stove had no fuel left.

Zeb put the frozen tin of beans in his pocket. He hoped the heat of his body might melt them so he could eat them.

Zeb got on the sled. He hurt all over.

"Mush! Mush!" Zeb yelled.

The dogs pulled hard and the sled moved off. Most times Zeb would help the dogs get started by running behind the sled. Today he rode the sled and the dogs had to work even harder to pull it. Zeb felt bad – bad for the dogs, bad for his parents, and bad for himself.

Zeb was hurt. He was out of food and out of fuel. His radio was broken and he had 200 miles of snow and ice to go before he got to the end of the race.

"It can't get any worse," he said to himself.

But it could.

Chapter 7
Hero?

The next two days were like a bad dream. Zeb and his dogs were hungry and tired. Zeb clung to the sled. Every breath hurt.

At last, Zeb saw log cabins ahead. He knew that meant he was getting near Nome – the end of the race.

Zeb felt hope for the first time. His team was going to make it!

Then Zeb felt the dogs getting slower. He felt angry. Why were they stopping?

"Mush!" he yelled. "Come on, Nukka!"

But Nukka did not move. She growled softly.

Zeb looked up and what he saw made him feel sick.

A polar bear was watching them.

Zeb knew that polar bears were often seen near Nome. They stole food and ate from dustbins. They hunted and killed dogs. Sometimes they killed people. They were fast and deadly. They were born hunters. And they were afraid of no one.

Zeb got his gun and tried to load the bullets. His hands shook badly.

Nukka growled in fear and anger and then started to bark. The other dogs were in a panic. They wanted to get away, but they were tied to the sled.

Then the polar bear charged.

Nukka snapped her ropes and sprang at the bear. She was a big, strong dog.

But the polar bear was bigger. Much, much bigger. The fight could not last for long.

The bear's long claws tore at Nukka. She yelped. The snow turned red with her blood.

"No! Please, no!" Zeb yelled. He fired his gun at the bear. He knew the bullets could not hurt the bear, but the noise might drive it away.

Zeb walked towards the bear, firing shot after shot. He didn't care if he lived or died. He had to save Nukka.

The bear roared at Zeb as it backed away. Then it turned and ran.

Zeb raced over to Nukka. Her eyes were closed but she was still alive. When he stroked her, her eyes opened and she licked his hand.

"Nukka! I'm sorry! Please don't die! We're nearly there! Hold on!" Zeb cried.

Zeb stumbled and cried as he put Nukka on the back of the sled.

The 7 other dogs pulled hard and the sled began to move.

An hour later, Zeb crossed the finish line in Nome. He wasn't the winner but he was the youngest musher to ever finish the Iditarod. A huge cheer went up from the crowd. Zeb saw his mum and dad running towards him.

"We knew we'd find you here!" they shouted.

Then they saw the look on Zeb's face.

"Help Nukka," was all he could say.

Zeb's dad ran to the sled. "I'm sorry, son," he said. "Nukka is dead."

The people of Nome gave Zeb a hero's welcome. But Zeb didn't care. Nukka was dead.

Two days later, Zeb, his parents and the other dogs travelled home.

"Nukka gave her life for you," Zeb's dad said. "That's how much she loved you. You were all she cared about."

"If I hadn't done this stupid race, she'd still be alive," said Zeb.

Zeb's dad nodded. "I know. And you'll have to live with that for ever. But you'll never forget Nukka. She saved your life. Dogs are like that. Treat them well and they'll always be loyal."

He looked at Zeb. "Your mum and I thought this might make you feel better." He put a small box into Zeb's hands.

Inside the box there was a husky puppy, curled up in a bed of straw.

"She's called Buniq," Zeb's dad said. "It means 'sweet daughter'."

Zeb smiled, but there were tears on his cheeks as he stroked Buniq's warm fur.

Our books are tested
for children and young people by
children and young people.

Thanks to everyone who consulted on
a manuscript for their time and effort in
helping us to make our books better
for our readers.